Bear Takes a Trip
Oso se va de viaje

Stella Blackstone
Debbie Harter

Bear has a very long journey to make.
There are lots of things for him to take.

Oso va a hacer un largo viaje.
Hay muchas cosas que tiene que empacar.

He makes his bed and washes his face.
He eats his breakfast and packs his case.

Hace la cama y se lava la cara.
Desayuna y empaca su maleta.

**He hops on the bus at the end of the lane.
It takes him through town, where he'll get
on the train.**

Se sube al autobús al final de la calle,
que lo lleva por el pueblo, donde se subirá
al tren.

He meets his friend, who is going too.
They chat about everything they want to do.

Se encuentra con su amigo, que va también.
Conversan sobre todo lo que quieren hacer.

At the railway station, they have to wait.
The train to the mountains is always late.

En la estación de trenes, tienen que esperar.
El tren a las montañas siempre se retrasa.

**Here it comes! The bears find their seats.
They open their picnics and share some treats.**

¡Ahí viene! Los osos encuentran sus asientos.
Sacan sus almuerzos y comparten golosinas.

They race out of town and follow the coast.
Bear can't decide which sights he likes most.

Salen del pueblo y bordean la costa.
Oso no puede decidir qué lugares le gustan más.

At long last, the journey comes to an end.
Bear has a cabin and so does his friend.

Por fin, el viaje ha terminado.
Oso tiene una cabaña y su amigo también.

The bears learn to sail on a mountain lake.
They also go climbing and they get back late.

Los osos aprenden a navegar en un lago
en la montaña.
También van de escalada y regresan tarde.

**They have lots of fun, whatever the weather.
Bear wants to stay here forever and ever!**

Se divierten mucho, sin importar el estado del tiempo.
¡Oso quiere quedarse aquí para siempre!

What Time Is It?

Nine o'clock
9:00 am

Ten past nine
9:10 am

Twenty past nine
9:20 am

Five to ten
9:55 am

Quarter to ten
9:45 am

Half past nine
9:30 am

¿Qué hora es?

Las nueve en punto
9:00 a.m.

Las nueve y diez
9:10 a.m.

Las nueve y veinte
9:20 a.m.

Las diez menos cinco
9:55 a.m.

Las diez menos cuarto
9:45 a.m.

Las nueve y media
9:30 a.m.

Vocabulary / Vocabulario

time – el hora
morning – la mañana
noon – el mediodía
afternoon – la tarde
evening – la noche
midnight – la medianoche
second – el segundo
minute – el minuto
hour – la hora
day – el día

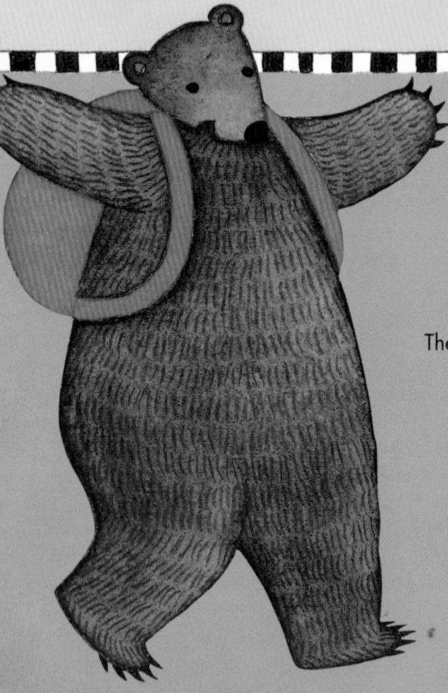

Barefoot Books
294 Banbury Road
Oxford, OX2 7ED

Barefoot Books
2067 Massachusetts Ave
Cambridge, MA 02140

First published in Great Britain by Barefoot Books, Ltd
and in the United States of America by Barefoot Books, Inc in 2011
This bilingual Spanish edition first published in 2013

Graphic design by Judy Linard, London and Louise Millar, London
Reproduction by B & P International, Hong Kong
Printed in China on 100% acid-free paper
This book was typeset in Futura and Slappy
The illustrations were prepared in paint, pen and ink, and crayon

ISBN 978-1-84686-945-7

British Cataloguing-in-Publication Data:
a catalogue record for this book is available from the British Library

Library of Congress Cataloging-in-Publication Data
is available upon request

Translated by María Pérez

1 3 5 7 9 8 6 4 2